VENI VIDI AMAVI

We came. We saw. We *loved*

VENI VIDI AMAVI

By Arisha Anne
Bhattacharya

At a touch of love, everyone becomes a poet.

To you

I hope you get everything you want in life, especially *love*, the kind

that's been sacrificed for you and the kind I hope you never stop

wanting.

I write to see my emotions scattered in ink,

Only then can one truly make words transform into life

Songs to fall in love to:

♥

1. La Vie En Rose–Édith Piaf

2. Those Eyes–New West

3. Dandelions–Ruth B.

4. Moment–Vierre Cloud

5. Just the Two of Us–Bill Withers and Grover Washington, Jr

6. Little Talks–Of Monsters and Men

7. Shut Up and Dance–Walk the Moon

8. My Love Mine All Mine–Mitski

9. Young and Beautiful–Lana Del Rey

10. Je te laisserai des mots - Patrick Watson

11. Can't Help Falling In Love–Elvis Presley

12. Golden Hour–JVKE

13. Locked Out of Heaven–Bruno Mars

14. Electric Love– BØRNS

15. Paper Rings–Taylor Swift

16. Make You Mine–PUBLIC

17. Somewhere Only We Know–Keane

18. I Wanna Be Yours–Arctic Monkeys

19. Tongue Tied–GROUPLOVE

20. Hey, Hey, Hey Lover - The Daughters of Eve

21. Sofia–Clario

Écrivant Notre Avenir

"If it isn't a happy ending yet, keep writing."

I've never stopped writing.

Some laugh at the absurdity of writing your feelings out

Carcasses of pens, husks of journals and backs of math books

Covered in scribbles of our interactions,

Kisses of happiness on the best days

Tears running the ink on the worst

Sometimes, happy endings are written on old discarded notes,

Crumpled tissue paper left in pockets,

Whiteboards erased in minutes

Note apps on my phone, forgotten within a week

Sometimes happy endings, or hope for them, are written in texts

Written in love letters, rewritten a hundred times

Written on their skin, written on tables,

Carved into your skin

But words contain meaning,

Keep writing till it comes true,

Or at least keep writing till you reach peace

Until your fantasies become reality

And reality ceases to be just words on a page

- *a sense of actively shaping and composing the narrative of what lies ahead*

Vellichor

There's more love in bookstores than chapels,

More forbidden tales between shelves than over balconies,

More written confessions between pages of a romance novel than on

Valentine's Day, for there is a strange phenomenon in bookstores

To be surrounded by a million lives and stories

Ones you wish to live, fantasies and myths crafted through imagination

and wishes, Such as the dreams you hate awaking from,

Narratives of falling in love;

Staying in love

Used bookstores hold a charm of a past donated anew,

Someone once held the book you thumb through,

Crying, laughing, experiencing it the same way you now do

Maybe it's the wistfulness of imagining another soul loving this story

Connected through words on a page,

Inscriptions promising joy and happiness left behind,

Annotations of hearts and frowns litter the page,

"My favourite moment!"

A small glance into the minds of those before you

A bookstore sees more love stories than anywhere on Earth,

A myriad of stories unsaid but written,

All in hopes of another picking it up and living it with them

the strange wistfulness of used bookstores

Arisha Anne Bhattaharya

Just for once

I'd like to be the poem

Not the poet

-

Ars Longa, Vita Brevis

"I wish I was a poem"

How do you know you're not

A stranger could've seen you walking

Wind in your face, hair stuck on your scarf,

Laughing so hard

That they fell in love with the second of the sound

Your friend still smiles back at compliments you gave them on a

bad day

Someone still giggles remembering a joke you said

Someone admires you enough to make you their goals

From all this

The love you give off to the world

Comes the birth of inspiration

The sweetness you bring in life

Will always make you someone's poetry

Art is long, life is short

Venostias

He was poetry in a world still learning the alphabet

He was everything beautiful,

The kind of poetry that brings tears to your eyes

World-changing, emotionally shattering

The kind that confuses you until reread a thousand times

The kind read out loud on stage, winning awards for talent and grace

He is a well-composed poem

The cursive flowing on the page,

The lyrics of a sonnet can sing out

The rhythm, the rhyme

The symphonies and melodies that torment my mind

Playing repeatedly on a loop

The strings of my heart strumming along to his pleasure

Till they snap

Loveliness

Una Anima, Duo Cor

Soulmates are just

Best friends who happened to fall in love

One soul, two hearts

Arisha Anne Bhattaharya

Elysian

You laugh like a bubbling brook,

Joyful ripples in every nook.

It's as if sunlight dances on the sea,

A gleaming horizon, wild and free.

A cascade of mirth, a radiant sunbeam

Akin to a songbird's morning tune,

Notes that kiss the heart, a sweet monsoon

It sounds like the promise of tomorrow

And an infinity of happiness

-    *something beautiful, divine, or idyllic*

Oubaitori

Spring is the love of

Keeping a rose from the bouquet given

Just so you know when to buy her flowers again

When yours wilts

-     *everyone grows and blooms at their own pace*

Apricate

Summer is the love of

Bringing extra sunscreen,

To dab it on their scrunched up noses

And laugh at their cheeks become red,

Not from the sun's love,

But yours

- *to sunbathe or bask in the sun*

Cryogonet

Winter is the love of

Wanting to never wake up on Christmas morning

Because the only gift you'd ever want

Huddled against the cold, lost in the snowflakes

Is lying in your arms

    _ *The winter wistfulness brought upon by the wisping winds of a snowy evening*

Psithurism

Autumn is the love of

Knowing all the flowers will die

And seeing the chill set in

But still falling for you anyways

   ⁻ *The whispering of leaves moved by the winds*

Summisse

I love grass stains on my shirts,

My skirts and pants are dotted with bright green and brown,

Weeds sticking in my hair and socks,

Flowers tumbling out of my pockets,

The scent of rain and acorns hits the air as I reopen my bags

I love the feeling of wet mud and grass underneath me,

Laying my head on bark and your chest,

Hearing the birds sing and your heart beat against my cheek

Grabbing stems, slowly picking off petals as your hands dance over my skin

The same dance the squirrels and foxes do over our heads

And as a drop of rain falls against my cheek,

So do your lips.

- *Softness of spring*

Ab imo pectore

You'd point out flowers to me,

"It's beautiful", I'd say

You just didn't know I was looking at your hands

From the bottom of the heart

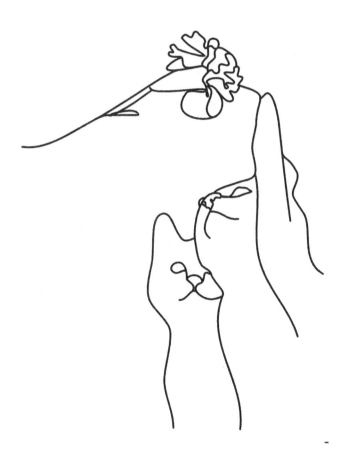

-

Arisha Anne Bhattaharya

Μέτρον βίου το καλόν ου το του χρόνου μήκος.

I hope seeing purple flowers

The oldest books in a library

The scent of caramel

An old trail no one walks

Long earrings and vintage bracelets

Or hearing a word no one uses

Seeing an owl outside your window

Or bright red boots

The cursive scribble on a love letter

An forlorn pinecone

Or knee high socks

They remind you of me

I hope these are the things you carry with you

Not the sharp words I left you with

*The measure of life is its beauty
not its length.*

Lagniappe

I hope when I die,

The flowers are purple,

The kind planted in your backyard, the kind picked up on our walks,

the kind sneakily placed into my hair.

I hope you remember to buy flowers.

I hope they are lavender and remind you of me when they linger on

your jacket afterwards.

I hope every time you see the colour purple,

My name floats through your mind like a soft symphony, a leftover

touch, a fleeting hope.

I hope I get flowers

And you realise that

In the same way, funerals see more flowers than dates

Hospitals hear more "I love you's" than churches

Airports see more tears and hugs than fancy restaurants

Because regret is so much stronger than appreciation

-   *A special kind of gift*

Οὐδὲν ἔρωτος ἄτοπον

Perhaps atoms resist their fusion's tether,

Two humans, never truly becoming one together

Yet when we met,

Somewhere, somehow,

our essences entwined; our souls became a reflection of each

other.

A reflection so captivating it could make him sigh,

The kind even Narcissus would die looking at

If only we learnt from history.

Flying too close to the sun,

Through risks untold, the thrill takes flight.

the excitement being merely as fragile as wax

Burnt the second we got too close,

Tumbling further than Icarus, beyond the bounds of time,

The rocks beneath us leaving scars on my heart,

Perhaps we should've ended there, choked by the waves till

our last breath,

Only to try pushing it back up,

Sisyphus's tragic tale being our wrongdoing,

never relenting, always bound to fail,

Maybe it was love or fear of normality's loss,

Crushing time and time again by that rock,

A struggle that seemed painless, a paradox.

-    *Nothing is absurd in love*

Should I never light a birthday candle,

For fear of dying from it's burn

Should I never step into an aeroplane,

For fear of never landing, landing in a fiery crash,

into a rock of waves, into bullets of rain,

Should I never speak,

For fear of losing my voice, never gaining back what I never

gambled

Never breathe, the first after drowning,

ever consuming, never big enough?

Never laugh, the earth-shattering kind, clutching your sides,

losing your breath?

Never smile, ear-to-ear, never abashed or shameful, teeth

shining, cheeks hurting from its joy?

For the fear of feeling it once and never again,

The haunting of its memory is worse than the prospect of never

holding it in my hands.

Should I never be in love?

Just for the fear of losing my heart,

Or putting back the pieces,

Like a mirror–never to be seen unless in chunks of its prior

beauty, cracks always visible,

a million versions of me staring back

Or should I be in love for the fear of never experiencing it?

Let it heal when it falls apart,

For love doesn't need bandages, the scribble of medication,

pills and injections.

All love needs is experience,

You'll always heal from living with love,

And die without letting it break you

Is it better to prevent than to heal?

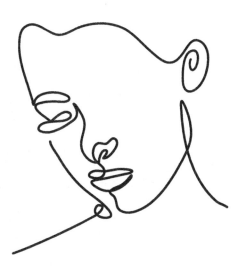

μεράκι

Do you regret it?

The stupid decisions, the rash comments, the scrambling conversations,

Foolish acts of forgiveness

Of compassion and delusion

The rushed confessions and sleepless nights arguing to fall back in love

The never-ending silences

The forlorn looks and unkempt emotions are never expressed

Do you ever regret doing it?

No, never

Why regret doing something for love?

When love is all we have to give to others

- *to do something with love*

Arisha Anne Bhattaharya

Verba volant, scripta manent

The way Gatsby bought a mansion just to hope Daisy

would stumble in one day and

See his heart coated in the luxury she craved

Perhaps the way Achilles killed hundreds for Patroclus

Wanting his love to bring back the dead

Or the way Darcy saved her sister without any recognition

To hope her realization would fall sooner than his obsession

These are how I hope to be loved

Beautiful enough to be written about

- *Words fly away, writings remain*

Hodie mihi, cras tibi

If today you work so hard for someone

Who gives you half their attention

Half their love

Imagine how beautiful a world it will be

When someone will give you their whole heart

Today it's me, tomorrow it will be you

La felicità è fatta di piccoli momenti

I never actually had a favourite animal

But when you "guessed" it

Excitement in your voice at the sheet coincidence,

I suddenly had one

- *happiness is made of small moments*

Kairosclerosis

My heart fluttered a millisecond too long,

Not wanting to hide my laugh anymore,

Smiling with my crooked teeth,

Making a joke that would've mortified me

My mind ran amok for a moment,

Diverting enough to make me forget my sadness

Just for a split moment when your face replaced it

Your voice replaced the sour taunt in my brain,

Soft like the ocean breeze

Sweet enough to help me swallow spoonfuls of salt without a second

thought.

The moment came when I began walking more quickly.

Mapping out my routes more than usual

Remembering your words more than normal

To feel the skip in my chest

Seeing your eyes once more

When I smiled properly for the first time in months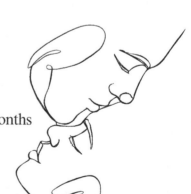

That's when I knew

Happiness didn't begin with an H

It began with you.

- *the moment when you realize you're happy*

Ichi-go ichi-e

The first night we met,

Your eyes twinkle against my glass, raising it away from my lips to

see the true you,

A first glance of a thousand,

A blush of a million as you nodded, a smirk dancing its tango on

your lips.

The same dance you'd ask my hand in an hour,

The same lips you'd laugh out of as we stumbled across the floor,

Having two left feet,

We danced till the night stopped feeling dark, until our feet stopped

touching the ground, floating through memories and introductions,

flirtatious lines and dirty jokes.

The way your fingers intertwined through mine, breaking the crowd

apart, guiding my blurred eyes and slurred words

Was it the alcohol or the high from the richness of your words that I kept

drinking?

Thirst starved, licking up anything leaving your mouth, hanging onto the

small mannerisms, sweet jokes,

The way you ruffled your hair, fixing it as I now do,

Tucking socks into your shoes, fiddling with your tie, your tongue

darting out to lick your parched lips,

Soon to be bright red and sticky

I remember it all too well,

Remember the exact moment I touched your cheek, flushed and hot

under me,

The tickle of your whisper in my ear, wishing your name into my

life, a curse of enchantment forever following our footsteps,

The moon's surface is a sandstorm swept away compared to

your imprints on my heart

Writing our story in each line,

A dance of souls, an intertwining sign.

- *one time, one meeting, an encounter that only happens once in*

  your life

Nubivagant

To live is to experience everything the world has to offer

To fall asleep on flights together,

Watching the sun rise over hills and clouds

Try new food, spoonfeed each other gelato or tiramisu

Dive into freezing currents and warm waves,

Holding hands paragliding, or falling from the sky as the world shifts

beneath us,

Grabbing your arm to not stumble on trains, tip off rickshaws, balance on

gondolas,

Running through grassy lands and forests filled with daisies

Taking daft pictures holding buildings,

Hour-long walks admiring architecture

In the city's embrace, time slows its pace.

Days spent wandering, a journey untold

Carried home when my feet gave out

Stuffing our luggage in to make space for presents and souvenirs,

Postcards, magnets, and memories abound.

Shirts hats matching, we stand tall,

In each other's company, we've it all.

To live, to love, to journey free,

In your company, my world, you see.

- *wandering through or amongst the clouds*

Amorevolous

Fall in love. It doesn't have to be with a person.

Fall in love with the smell of rain.

The small drops of leaves that shakedown on your face

in the dawn The orchestra of birds that wake you up

The twinkle of the stars

Or the moon's shine on your eyes

Fall in love with noise—hearing people talk about things they love, seeing the joy light up their faces, the excitement creep into their voices, rambling on and on

Fall in love with silence—the serenity of your room after a tough day, the quietness of an empty park, top of a mountain, sitting by the creek

Fall in love with paintings, with art, with music and stories— with everything crafted through the love of living and experiencing

Fall in love with learning.

With knowledge and exploration—with opening a book, stepping onto new soil, hearing another tale

Fall in love with living beings

A butterfly landing on your window

Your dog who loves you more than life itself

The small frogs balancing on waterlilies

The squirrels that watch you

Fall in love with conversations and first glances

Hi's and hello's

The sparks of new friendships

Fall in love with adrenaline

Surfing through waters unexplored

Running through the rain

Hiking higher than anyone

Fall in love with *anything* that makes you happy

The small pleasures in life

Because one day you'll wake up

And realize the little things in life

Were the biggest;

Your reasons for waking up

Fall in love with the things guaranteed to stick by you,

The beauty of living

- *loving*

Teiubesc

Je t'aime

Ik houd van jou

Ich liebe dich

Te quiero

Mahal kita

Aloha wau iā 'oe

我愛你

Te amo

Я тебя люблю

Σε αγαπώ

I feel the world's love in just one person

When I'm with you

- *I love you*

Με κάθε καρδιά που χτυπά, σε λέει όνομα
-

You're a language that I can't remember how to speak

But still understand even in my sleep

With every heartbeat, it says your name

Ἀπὸ τοῦ ἡλίου μετάστηθι

Looking into your eyes was a pleasure only a few knew

But watching them flutter close as you fell asleep

Seeing them soften into butter as you looked at me

The sly winks when no one is paying attention

That's the part of your soul revealed only by glancing at them

When you weren't looking.

- *The great pleasures come from watching beautiful deeds.*

Bellus

Brown things are such a beauty

Beneath the amber canopy, whispers of rust,

Coffee swirls like a tawny dream,

In the cup's warmth, memories gleam

A tree trunk older than us

deep pools of mahogany,

And your eyes

- *Beautiful*

Sguardo Incantevole

Your eyes betray you

Some say eyes are the windows to the soul

Yours aren't windows

They are an oculus in your thoughts,

Into the heavens of your emotions

The galaxies of your needs

They betray your words of ignorance and pity

Of nonchalance and anger

They betray you,

For who can look so in love with such a filthy mouth?

The way you look at me chokes me.

The blue was so deep

The endless ocean in your pupils

And should they pull me into the waves of adoration

Crashing constantly on my lips

I'd gladly drown a million times

- *The way you look at me*

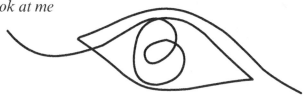

Γλαυκοίσιν οφθαλμοίσιν αιδώς ουκ ένι

I never loved the color blue

Until I saw you wear it everyday

And match my gaze

- *There is no shame in light blue eyes*

Cingulomania

When the first humans were made,

It was a pair, moulded together through fate

One body, two minds, two hearts,

Until the gods cut them apart, severing them forever,

Scattered across the world,

Left to spend their lives searching for their other half,

Legend says when found.

The puzzle is completed, fused together once more,

A perfect fit into each other's arms.

Never let go again.

"You fit into my arms a little too well"

My head in the crook of your neck,

Your hair tickling mine no less than your lips grazing my ears,

My arms wrapped around your neck, leaning up no more than

needed,

Yours around my waist, clutching tightly enough to make me hear

my heartbeat drum in my ear,

Mirroring yours

"Almost like you were made for me."

- *hold a person in your arms*

Fallacia

Oh darling

Feed me lies

Lies that are sweet, sickly sweet, as they drip off your tongue

Like honey to choke me, stolen from another to sweeten me up,

Pulling me under your embrace in a sticky mess

Spun in a cobweb of deceit and trickery

The kind I've grown addicted to spreading on my lips

- *Deceit*

Nitimur in vetitum

I hate you

I hate you with everything I have in me

Kiss me once more

And never talk to me again

- *We strive for the forbidden*

Mellifluous

You never looked more pretty

Than when you begged me

To let you go

I wish I did

Holding on made you fall for me all the more.

How you must have loved my hands on you

- *A sound that is sweet and smooth, pleasing to hear*

"Let's have some fun."

Stolen kisses when no one's looking

Brushed palms against my leg,

Whispered taunts, filthy promises, delusional promises

Why make it serious,

No need for love, hugs, sleeping in each other's arms

Fast breaks, rushed makeups, scribbled meet-ups and sleepless nights

instead

Escaping through windows, running out to meet in the middle,

Through concealed streets and foggy dawns,

Behind classrooms, inside cars, against my walls

What's the deal with emotions?

Messy feelings?

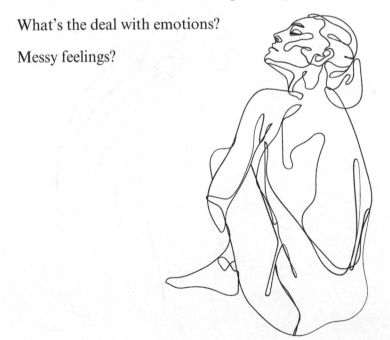

The only thing needed to be feeling

Is your hair against my neck,

Hands against my hips, nails against your back

Perhaps I'm being fanciful

But love stories are such a waste of time,

Riding on the tip of a knife,

Pressing it against your neck as more lies pour out

Playing with fire as water,

Racing hearts, buzzed minds, lost breaths and rash decisions

Sounds like such a better narrative than

"I fell in love."

- *I hate love stories*

Psychomachy

I hear your voices in my head

Whenever I start to move on

Begging me to stay behind

To wait

When all I am supposed to do is run,

Just like the voice in front of my face

Is telling me to do

\- *A battle for the soul*

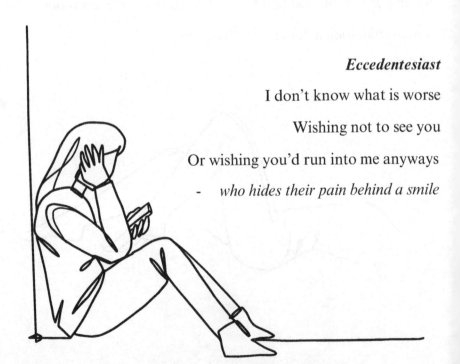

Eccedentesiast

I don't know what is worse

Wishing not to see you

Or wishing you'd run into me anyways

\- *who hides their pain behind a smile*

Veni Vidi Amavi

Iuxta

How close do you have to be to break

To burn from the sun's rays

To drown inside a whirlpool

To suffocate under poison

How close do you have to be until the feeling of ecstasy stops feeling

numbing?

Until I can't ignore the pain for a moment of solitude and happiness

One laugh for a nighttime of tears

One smile for an afternoon of hiding my eyes

One word for a lifetime of regret

How close is close enough to oblivion, never touching yet never

letting go

Constantly caught in the net you've knit, clutching me as if you can't

let go

Yet spitting venom every time I want to come closer

Is being too close bad? Is being far better?

Far enough so you forget me, forget the feeling of my presence,

forget the way my eyes would meet yours, and my hands would hold

your own

Far enough so it stops hurting every time I remember your name

Far enough to never bring me close to breaking again

- *Too close*

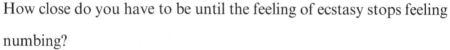

Vulnerant omnes, ultima necat

It's hard to break someone with all the things they hate

But so easy

When you broke me

In all the ways I loved you

- *They all wound, the last one kills*

Perdere omnia nisi animam

Why must I be sad?

I lost someone who didn't love me enough to put in the effort

You lost someone who loved you enough to go through the

hardships; all the effort, all the heartache—just for half a try at

happiness

Who lost more here?

The unloved or the unlovable

- *To lose all but one's soul*

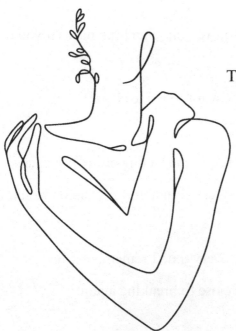

Scelero

Your words, like knives, cut through the air,

Leaving wounds that only time can repair.

A dance of pain, a tragic show,

How you must love seeing me weep for you

Is watching me fight for us not your favourite sight?

How many times must I say,

That same word, time and time again, just for you to break it. For

us to break it?

It doesn't matter whose lips they leave; it holds no meaning

anymore.

"Sorry"

Sorry for making me believe, for hoping, for praying, for wishing

upon every star that passes by, every eyelash that falls

Sorry for leading you on and giving you ideas and thoughts that were

wrong, deluded, false, or *fake.*

Sorry for our past, our messed up past that I keep forgetting, keep

glossing over just to make

The same mistake, time and time again

"It's ok."

Because you could stab my heart

And I'd still go down on my knees to apologise

For getting blood on your hands

- *to pollute with guilt, with blood*

Dictum factum

"I didn't mean to" falls short in the abyss,

Actions, the architects of trust or dis

"It's a misunderstanding."

A dance of misunderstanding, a tangled thread,

Words falter, and actions scream instead

Saying you didn't mean to stab me, yet whose hand is covered in

blood,

Whose knife is sticking out of my chest, covered in your excuses

"You're taking it the wrong way,"

Yet actions sculpt realities that words can't feed.

"That's not what I meant," a futile plea,

In the shadow of actions, intentions cease to be.

What did you mean to do then?

How many times can a kiss be misinterpreted as a sting

An adoring word be taken as black and white

When all it does is explode into colour inside my mind

How can a touch be made into a snap, a smile into a grimace?

Deeds, the canvas where integrity's painted,

Words, mere whispers, easily tainted

Actions speak, where words are undone.

- *What is said is done*

Δεσμεύομαι. *(Desmévomai)*

The only way to ensure promises

Are through the pinkies

Linking them, feeling your palms heat up under mine

As I swing our arms, still connected by a single promise

You never let go,

And perhaps I never did either

Which is why

When the promise did

My pinky broke, and yours merely splattered by the blood of

betrayal

- *I commit*

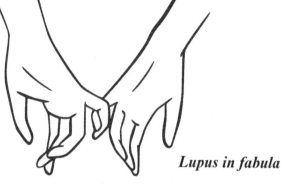

Lupus in fabula

Your wounds were something I'd stitch every day,

But when they started to match mine.

That's when your blood stopped coating my

hands,

And I let you bleed out.

- *The wolf in the story*

Odi et amo

I promise you this.

I'll never hate you the way you tried to make me.

For true hatred can't befall someone held dear;

you'll always hate the idea of them

The situation

The challenges

The actions

But never the person

Somewhere underneath all that turmoil

Is just the boy I fell in love with one rainy afternoon

- *I hate, and I love*

Εγώ σκόροδα σοι λέγω, συ δε κρόμμυα αποκρίνει

Isn't it funny

How you'd tell me I made you the happiest person on Earth

Just to never smile at me again

- *I talk to you about garlics and you respond about onions.*

Arisha Anne Bhattaharya

Amor Et Melle Et Felle Es Fecundissimus

"I hate you."

How can one's words be so cruel,

So harsh, so devoid of emotion

it doesn't even sound like you…

Filled only with fire

When it once was fueled with sugar

Honey coating every syllable, dripping off your lips,

Soothing, not stinging my own

How can it be?

Is that even you anymore?

Is your throat burnt with hatred,

Or did I light you on fire one too many times with boiling sugar

Did that sweetness taste bitter now?

-    *Love is rich with both honey and venom*

Ad hominem

Never did you speak the way you did today.

Was this side of you always there

Or does it come out when you fall out of love

- *aimed at the man*

Resistentia

Some say that infatuation comes close to obsession

I say infatuation comes close to *defiance*

Never admitting the truth

Never giving in to the facts presented

Who should?

Would you listen to your brain when your heart says otherwise?

Open defiance, angry words, arguments and insults,

Whispered screams and seething glares

Is it a sign of hate?

It would be, should it end with no more words,

Should it end in silence, it would be hatred

But

Should it end in sweet words, a repeat, a rerun,

Second chances

A hundred chances

Is that hatred, or is it infatuation?

Never leaving, never relenting, never giving up

Infatuation should be called defiance,

The same way love should be called hate.

- *Defiance*

Ira furor brevis est

Never has there been a word so sharp

That it causes a bead of blood to bubble to the surface

But for you?

I hope every sentence bleeds you to death.

- *Anger is a brief madness*

Ubi amor ibi dolour

My soul is tied to yours

So tightly knit that pulling it

Will bleed us both to death

Not bound by a thread

But iron

Yet why do you keep cutting it

Don't you realise the pain only gets worse with sharper edges?

- *When there is love, there is pain*

Νεφελώδης Αγκαλιά του Πελάγους

I wish I wouldn't cross oceans for someone who wouldn't cross a
puddle for me.

But isn't that the art of truly loving a person

Giving in even when reciprocation isn't there?

I thought this was the case,

Used it to justify his actions, the nonchalance, the blank stares and
meaningless thank-you's,

But *no,*

You should cross oceans for people who will cross the ocean
alongside you

Those who hold an umbrella for you in a storm

Those who guide you through the rain

Who picks you up when you can't walk

Read for you when your eyes hurt

Sing for you when your heart hurts

Someone who will listen when you ramble

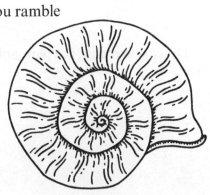

Not just hear you, but listen enamoured, hanging onto every word

Find someone who loves your stories and will recite them back to you

Someone who would cook your favourite meal,

Learn your favourite songs,

your language, your culture

Find someone who won't just be willing to cross an ocean for you but rather

Split the sea in half so that you don't get wet

- *Cloudy Embrace of the Sea*

Gunnen

You told me about the sea a thousand times,

Pointing out the currents,

the undulating rhythm of waves,

The abruptness of ocean storms,

The movement of crabs under our feet,

Taught me how the cliffs were formed,

The ammonite's histories,

Picking up seashells to keep,

Giving the most beautiful to each other

And as we amble along the shoreline,

The sand beneath our feet,

All too familiar of a feeling

I'll forget them,

I'll pretend I don't remember a thing,

Not to dismiss but to savour anew,

Just to hear you tell me all over again

The cadence of your voice, the sea in you.

To find happiness in someone else's happiness

Quiescence

When I first saw that smile

I knew the sun didn't matter anymore

I could sustain life

Just off making you happy

- *quiet happiness*

Quem plus illa oculis suis amabat

I knew I loved you.

When everything I hated about myself

Started being my favourite traits

Because they were *your* favourite traits

-*Whom she loved more than her eyes themselves*

Ἀπὸ τοῦ ἡλίου μετάστηθι

Love isn't always loud

You don't notice it like a train barreling towards you

But a paper boat rocking in rainy streets

The kind of love from a

Mother putting socks on you as you sleep

A father's encouraging words after a long day

A best friend never gets tired of taking pictures until you get the

right one

Just to see your smile perfectly light up the screen

As it does in real life

A lover's soft humming of your favourite song

One they never knew

But learnt from you

Quiet love is so beautiful

Not many people notice it

But when you do,

It becomes the loudest of them all

Forelsket

You were the beginning of so many beautiful things

And the end of the worst

- *the feeling you have when first falling in love*

Novalunosis

Remind me of the stars.

How they sparkle without me begging them

How they show up without my reminders

Their lights shining every single night

Without my tears reflecting off them,

Remind me how the stars love

And tell me why you can't be like them.

- *the state of relaxation and wonderment experienced when*

  gazing at the stars

Εὖ φιλεῖν, εὖ φιλεῖσθαι

The only reason I've ever believed in love

Is because of the way I love

To love and be loved is the best

Orphic

How funny it is

When others are blind to things, you notice

The quirks and idiosyncrasies, a hidden delight,

The sweetness and charm, a private affair,

Memories painted in hues only we share.

How can others understand what you see in them

The utter love and joy their presence radiate

Small smiles, words that breathe life back into the dullest days,

Touches that leave a trail of fire bigger than volcanoes

How to convey the surge of serotonin,

The sheer bliss, the highs they summon?

Words falter before the profundity of this sacred ground,

An unspoken language, in the heart, it's astoundingly found.

-    *mysterious and enchanting; beyond ordinary understanding*

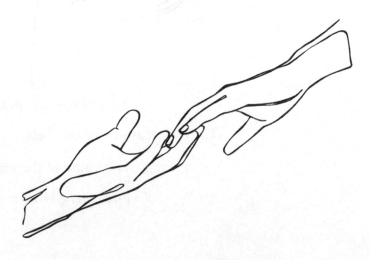

Agape

When I stop speaking around you

And let silence envelop us

To the only sounds being our breaths and heartbeats

That's when you know all my thoughts and memories.

That's when we stop becoming.

And fully being

A seamless blend of you and me.

- *the highest form of love*

Ορατή Αγάπη, Άφαντη Ιστορία

I wish to leave such a mark on you

That anyone who knows you after

Will have to know me

In order to love you

- *Visible Love, Invisible Story*

Cordiform

When we're stressed, to feel your head on my shoulders

Driving home and feeling your hand touch mine,

When you call me right after waking up, a drowsy voice so deep and

soft,

The heavens' clouds would be jealous

Every wave, every glance, every nod across the room when no one sees

your gaze but me. When you sing, and I along,

Voice cracks, high pitches, low laughs just to finish the song,

Listening to you talk for hours,

Every voice memo, every long walk, rushed recaps between classes,

Experiencing your life through memories, hoping to feel you before I

even knew you,

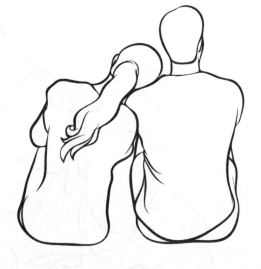

Breaking apart from a hug to feel your fingers still hover over their place on my hips,

Pulling me back in when my eyes roam your lips

The teasing smiles I trace with my tongue, the lipgloss marks left on your shirt,

Messy hair, crumpled shirts, a drunk smile

No thoughts were left behind but your name,

When your eyes glass over and you speak of the future,

Our future, weaving a tale so beautiful

The fates would cry from envy

Those small times when life stops being black and white, right and wrong, but merely,

Heart-shaped <3

Vorfreude

Deep within a bustling city,

Or perhaps a quiet farm in the middle of nowhere

Pushing our kids up the stairs,

Hot coffee warming up my hands as you bring it to bed

In the glow of a bedside lamp's soft light,

Moments stitched together every day and night.

Our golden gently snoring by the window, soft rain pattering

outside, A symphony of laughter, joy, and cares

For in these simple, ordinary scenes,

Vorfreude blooms like perennial greens

Dotting each other's noses with flour and sugar,

Painting the walls, hanging up your work

As they explode with colour and recollection,

Our pictures hung on the mantle, magnets littering the fridge

A library holding thousands,

Leading to a backroom kept a secret, just for our company

A studio, red and pink on the walls, blue and green in your

hair.

They match your eyes; I laugh, earning a splatter of purple on

mine

In a house we designed, covered in the memories of our past,

How beautiful of a future envisioned

- *(joyful) anticipation of the future pretences*

Songs for falling out of love:

♥

22. Sweater Weather–The Neighborhood

23. Moral Of The Story– Ashe

24. War of Hearts–Ruelle

25. Romantic Homicide–d4vd

26. K. –Cigarettes After Sex

27. We Don't Talk Anymore–Charlie Puth

28. The Night We Met–Lord Huron

29. Atlantis–Seafret

30. I Love You So–The Walters

31. Let You Break My Heart Again–Laufey and Philharmonia Orchestra

32. Till Forever Falls Apart–Ashe and FINNEAS

33. Memories–Conan Gray

34. Fourth of July–Sufjan Stevens

35. Someone Like You–Adele

36. It Must Have Been Love–Roxette

37. Watercolor Eyes–Lana del Ray

38. Two Birds– Regina Spektor

39. Blue Hair– T.V. Girl

40. Gilded Lily–Cults

41. Jealousy Jealousy–Olivia Rodrigo

Οι αναμνήσεις καίνε όταν η αγάπη εξαφανίζεται

You'll become a memory, a fleeting thought about a boy

I once knew

someone I once loved

You'll become another name, another picture never opened, a

text never returned

a conversation I'd have once killed to have

You'll cease to make me smile; your name will have no meaning

besides four letters

Your face will blend into the crowd, and my eyes will stop endless

searching for your hair

Your jacket, your bag, your voice

while I wait around just to glance at you once now, for one

look is enough to brighten my day

I'll forget your words, the way you speak, the way you sing and

laugh

The way your mouth turns up when you talk about painting and

physics and fishing

The way your eyes light up when you laugh at my jokes, stupid as

they are

I'll forget the daft inside jokes, the references and comments once

engraved within my brain

Arisha Anne Bhattaharya

how I wish to hear them one more time

You'll become a memory,

And the thought of your eyes, your lips, your touch and scent

Your foolish promises and praises, your ideas and lies of the future,

Will stop stinging and merely turn into a scar

but right now, you still bleed through me every single day

and how I wish for you to become just

a memory.

\-   *Memories burn when love disappears*

Semper anticus

How can you force time to rearrange itself

To turn back, it's arms to yesterday

Just for another chance at a future already written in stone.

How can you ask for time to slow down

When all he does is speed it up

Time has no reason to change,

Just like you have no reason to change

What's coming will inevitably come,

Just as the memories will inevitably fade

Let time take its toll

And always move forward

- *always forward*

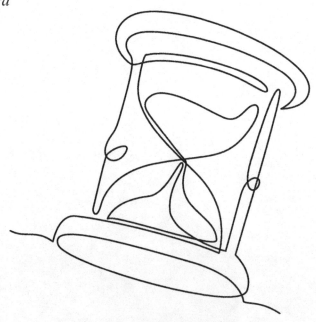

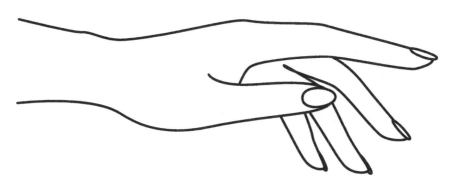

Omnia Mea Mecum Porto

I love the way I remember memories

Like a tape played back again and again

To just close my eyes

And be reliving that day once more

Perhaps that's why I'm stuck in those memories

Ones that feel too much like

Going back in time

I carry all my things with me

Retrouvaille

I'd choose you

In duststorms

Blizzards and murky waves

Through freezing winters and scorching summers,

Even blind or deaf

Mute or numb

I'd choose you when I know nothing of the future

When my footprints are indistinguishable,

I can't see my hand in front of my face.

I'd choose you.

The only road forward I need to memorize

\-   *meeting again after a long time*   **παράκοσμος**

Perhaps in another life

We could laugh at the prospect of not loving each other in this one

- An imaginary universe

Limerence

Some people are lucky enough to fall in love once.

I was lucky enough to fall in love every single day,

Through every small moment

Those late-night conversations

One strum of your guitar

The sweet melody of your voice

A joke you remembered

Or the coffee you brought me after a long night

A kiss on the cheek before running off

Or a hug goodnight

Those little moments

Day after day

Make me fall in love with you all over again

-    *The state of being infatuated with another person*

Effervescent

I hated dancing,

Until your hand led the way

And the music began to match the beat of our hearts

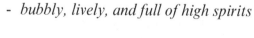

- *bubbly, lively, and full of high spirits*

Querencia

After a long day,

It feels good to come home

Home where I can take off my shoes without the ground hurting

my feet

Home where I can take off my clothes without feeling embarrassed

Home where I can speak without stuttering over my words

Overthinking each line as if on record

Home where the scent of hot cookies, lavender tea and ham

sandwiches meet me as I walk in,

Home where the bed floats like clouds,

My dreams are starting to twist reality

Home, which embraces me so warmly that the sun stops feeling hot

A blanket never to emerge from

A home that's lit up 24 by 7

Never blackouts, only dimming as sleep overtakes us

After a long day,

It feels good to come home

It feels good to come to you

- *a place from which one's strength is drawn, where*
  one feels at home

In perpetuum et unum diem

I'll always leave the light on

Throughout the night, the only one left flickering on the

street long after everyone's gone Keep the door ajar,

Even in the winter,

Snowflakes whisper tales, a quiet descent,

Raindrops dance, a clandestine lament.

Mist weaves illusions, a veiled ballet,

Hail, the percussion in a symphony astray

Within these walls, echoes of yesteryear

Destroying the furniture, staining the carpets, breaking

windows

Ajar, it lingers, a heart exposed

I'll leave it open for you

Return if you want

When you may decide, slowly slipping into the ruins yet

I hope the door hasn't been ripped off its hinges,

Or the light burnt out

May you find your way through time's cruel art,

To a home where the door is still ajar

- Forever and one day

Defenestration

I wish one day when you return

I'll bang the door on your face

Like you did me

But beyond all the harsh words and fake threats

I know the second you show up at my doorstep

You'll enter.

- *the act of throwing someone out of a window*

Ad astra per aspera

January is always a lovesick month.

Moving onto a new heart,

With the strings of yesterday still being pulled out

To the stars through difficulties

Razbliuto

Did you ever delete my pictures

Or do you go back on lonely nights

To remember how

Once

Forever ago

You didn't need my pictures to see my face

Or my videos to hear my voice

How calm of a world

Before you let me go

- *the sentimental feeling you have about someone you once*

 loved but no longer do

Memoria Nobis Vita Est

When I thought of our future

Looking back at our photos

Smiling at the start

Laughing at the foolish things we did

Softly leaning my head on your shoulder sharing stories

This is what I believed it would be

Us looking back at memories

Not us becoming a memory

- *Memory is life for us*

Sufficientia

For true greatness, it is never "good enough."

With "good enough," the car may stall,

Ambitions crumble, high hopes fall

The echoes of doubt, a relentless stream,

A haunting whisper, a recurring theme.

A single misstep, a fragile thread,

Unseen, but felt in the words left unsaid.

Always left questioning if an action was correctly secretly

mistaken

A word spelt wrong ending to tear apart the whole book

The colour of my lips shone too bright under the sun, enough

to blind his eyes.

Turn them away in one glance

Was it not good enough, this flawed rendition?

A moment's imperfection, a silent admission.

Perhaps good enough is just the act of existence,

Not trying harder, looking prettier, acting sweeter,

One could be the best package of all time

Packed with the hope of the future,

Love of the past

Dreams spanning infinity

Yet could still be futile, thrown away, discarded

If delivered to the wrong address

- *good enough*

Ira excusat errorem

I'd always kill for you

Or die for you

But for once,

I wish you'd just live for me

\- *Anger excuses error*

Cessante causa, cessat effectus

When I take one step forward,

You take one back,

Yet the second my eyes flit away, your hands grab me, yearning my

attention again.

You say you don't need me,

Yet your words call me, like a butterfly to nectar, drowning itself

until its wings are broken and wet from the sweetness.

A delicate tension, a yearning embraced.

One moment distant, the next entwined,

A dance of the heart, both yours and mine

Your hands inch towards mine, yet grabbing them is wrong, a sin

Perhaps it's only a sin when the devil commits it,

And not your false idea of angelic behaviour

When your eyes catch mine, staring across a room, following my figure,

How am I supposed to know you meant to stare at my shoes, the book in my arm,

The walls behind me,

You meant to compliment my brain, not my hair,

my ability to walk correctly, and not my legs.

You meant to show friendship when calling me at midnight,

saying my name over and over like a mantra

You'd meant not to give wrong signs,

painting it red when it was green

Perhaps I'm colourblind

Or you're blind to the reality everyone else sees

- *With removed, the effect ceases*

Quandary

We ignore

We act surprised when it happens

Because sometimes

Our brains know the answer

But our hearts can't accept it

- *A state of perplexity or uncertainty, especially as to what to do*

Quos Amor Verus Tenuit, Tenebit

I'll never leave you,

But don't ever expect me to hold onto a hand

That wants to leave

So, be rest assured,

I won't sever our ties,

but I won't be shackled to expectations, either

\-   *love will hold onto those it has held*

Sine qua non

For me to shut you out

When my heart was always open for you

Says a lot about the way you treated me

- Without which, not

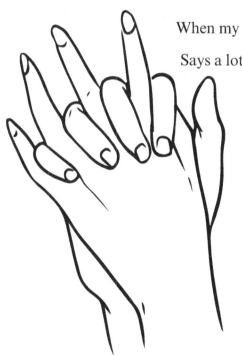

Arisha Anne Bhattaharya

Mamihlapinatapai

5 hours spent picking my red dress,

The nails matched perfectly,

the exact shade my lip bled later when my teeth stabbed them.

Watching you walk away,

the red lighting up my cheeks in embarrassment,

The hue of confusion,

Anger, sadness, envy,

A red dress that fit too perfectly to feel claustrophobic

It stuck to my skin, taking all of my power not to rip it off me after seeing your

eyes roam it, Temptation hungry enough within your gaze,

Yet, restraint enough to break mine, not wanting to meet the blue waters you

held

For fear of drowning, never feeling my skin again without remembering your

fingers skimming them

The same fingers now so far,

Breaking promises of grasping mine, dancing with the red glittering through

the rain,

Our colours match; isn't that funny?

Colours and the faraway looks, two birds of a feather

In the rain's glitter, our colours merge,

A silent dance, a bittersweet surge.

- A look shared by two people, each wishing that the other would initiate

something they both desire, but which neither wants to begin

Sakujo

Looking back at the photos,

My memories of a girl once so naive, so young, so foolish,

It's easy to forget,

Easy to criticise and ridicule

Easy to point fingers and wish the past was different,

To rip them apart as if the evidence would erase the memory

"How could I have done that?"

Deleting them is easy: one button, two clicks, a swipe close to

wiping its existence clean.

Do the memories hurt less when you don't see them?

Can I even go through them without scrolling faster, not wanting

to glimpse your smile through the blurs?

Is that why you deleted them, too?

To get rid of the pain

Or perhaps get rid of the version of yourself associated with me

_   *the act of removing or eliminating something, including the*

concept of deleting someone or something

Anagapesis

I used to search for things that reminded me of you

Your favourite colour,

A joke you'll laugh at

An experience you'd love to have; we'd love to have together.

Now all I can do is avoid them

- *no longer feeling any affection for someone you once loved*

Expectations

To be let down by your actions.

Being forced to embrace the disappointing realities which make

my mind break apart is one thing.

It's not you who hurt me, a profound decree,

But the shadows of expectations haunting me

Expecting devotion

Wanting apologies

Needing change

Receiving nothing but empty promises, half-baked praise, and

bored stares,

It's the expectations that slowly wane.

The version of you in my head, a ghost, now gone

The kind I expected to materialise before me

Shattered my heart more than this reality's actions

For in letting go of what I thought you'd be,

I can embrace who you've become

-   *Someone not worthy of my expectations*

Viridity

How many time will we excuse bullet wounds

Just because we love the one behind the trigger

- *Naive innocence*

Serpens in corde

If a heart is truly made to be broken

Then don't let it

Burn it instead,

Watch the flames burst through,

Charing them to cinders,

All who defy the true meaning of love

Let it ruin souls,

Tear consciousness apart

Snap heartstrings

Absolutely kill whatever little empathy was left,

For if being in love is the epitome of emotional value

And having emotions makes us human

Why would anyone want them?

Being human is being compassionate, empathetic, being vulnerable.

Such weakness

Why let love ruin you,

When you can ruin everyone who forces these rose colored lens on you?

- *Serpent in the heart*

Tanhai

Was I waiting for you?

Or was I looking to stop the growing loneliness that your absence

left?

Did I truly need your words, your praise, your gifts and your kisses

Or did I need someone to love me the way I loved others

Just to see reciprocation for the first time

Was it you I sought, or a mirror to reflect,

The broken dreams of a future planned out, of waking up to pure

happiness, not questions.

Were you the missing piece, or just a room?

A space for love to find its rhyme,

Did the loneliness you replaced find its place too fitting in my heart

A void that no new chapter triggers.

Did you unknowingly displace what was known?

Loneliness finding a perch, its throne.

For you came at the perfect time,

Only for your leaving to never fit into any version of my life

following it

- loneliness

Verisimilitude

I loved the idea of you so much that

An idea was all it took to break my reality

- *The appearance of being true or real*

Chagrin

Why can't you heal?

Get over the pain and the memories that haunt you every day,

Wipe the slate clean,

Leave them behind, an instance of time, a figure of my past

Just another name to add to the millions?

"Why do you keep it alive?"

Alive to keep breaking you apart,

alive enough to beat louder than your heart,

alive to keep speaking over your brain

alive to make you choke on your words,

erase any rational thought and obliterate

any self-preserving

"Tell me why?"

Because sometimes,

Pain is the closest thing left to love; there is.

And without the pain of love,

What's left to live for in life?

- *the notion of holding onto pain, expressing a sense of sorrow*

  or distress

Aquila non capit muscas

I hope if I ever get the chance to treat you

The way you treated me

I'll be half as merciful

And leave you with half a heart left

- *An eagle does not catch flies*

Basorexia

Kiss me

Kiss me until you can't breathe anymore

The only life you need

Being your name balancing on my lips,

Your tongue guiding my words

And my hand choking your thoughts

- *un baiser*

Fac et Spera

Change is inevitable, failure is inevitable, uncertainty is inevitable

You can't stop it; another's actions, thoughts, life.

You can't change opinions or perspectives,

Can't change prejudice and hate

All you can do is hope,

Go on, go and hope for a better future,

Run into the rain, fall through a cloud, hug a tree, dance in empty fields, in

bustling roads,

Let your hair down, your insecurities and doubts, let it go

What could possibly happen? Refusal?

Or holding onto regret, the pain of not knowing, the "what ifs" and "what not."

Tell them those three fated words; fated for destruction and pain

Fated for lust and heartburn

Fated for happiness and loneliness

But how would you know?

Know the seas that lay under the cliff; a rocky demise or a dream of coral reefs,

a world waiting patiently for you

Just take the plunge

Hold your hand out to the storm and hope lightening doesn't burn you

through,

Kiss the thorns and hope the red of roses, not blood, stains your lips,

Do what makes you hope in life,

For without hope, how can anything be worth fighting for?

- *do and hope*

Ikigai

Perhaps you're not my first

Not my first kiss or my first *I love you,*

Not the first date or the first all-nighter,

But you were the first person

Who actually made an "I love you."

Feel worth saying.

- *That which gives your life worth, meaning, or purpose.*

Audeamus

Dare we dance in love's fierce flame,

As roses bloom 'midst thorns unseen,

Let daring be our chosen sheen.

In the labyrinth of passion's glare,

Audeamus, our emblem rare

- *let us dare*

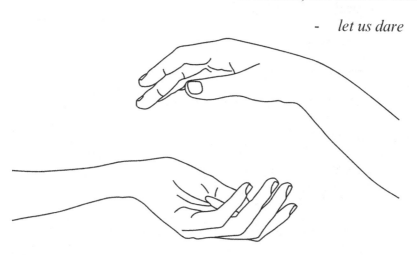

Arisha Anne Bhattaharya

Dulce periculum

It's a bad idea right?

Seeing you tonight,

Sending that one text that leads to more,

Watching each flirty tone escalate,

Knowing in the morning, we'd both live to regret it

But at the devil's hour,

No one awake to hear my sighs, your gasps, my chuckles, your sweet

nothings,

It definitely isn't a good idea to say your name out loud,

To hear you whisper mine back

To fool reality for a moment,

Suspended in a needle of time where

Just for a mere minute,

Everything is perfectly aligned,

The moon's disapproval, the stars' questions, the wind's objections

All fall on deaf ears as we spend the night,

Forgetting our pasts,

Ignoring the future–leaving just the gnawing nudge at our conscience, the

pinpricks of issues left unsolved, the arguments waiting to ensue

3 am. 3 words.

A million regrets in the morning, but

Nothing short of indulgence at this moment.

But isn't life meant to be a bit of a bad decision anyway?

-    *Danger is sweet*

ἄπαξ λεγόμενον

A million thoughts, a million chances.

Yet once uttered, echoes in the air,

Irrevocable, a weight to bear.

But once said,

It can never be taken back,

Maybe I'm not ready for one last shot after all.

The cost is too high, and the consequences are

fraught.

The bullet of words, a dangerous art

Shattering not just the silence but the heart,

A delicate masterpiece torn apart.

I once uttered, a cascade irreversible.

A million thoughts were captured, yet worlds apart.

- "*Once said*" *A word that only occurs once*

Cogitationis poenam nemo patitur

and so I must always be cursed

to write you letters that I can never send

- *No one suffers punishment for mere thoughts*

I miss you, I type.

No, I don't, I say.

How can you miss tsunamis, hurricanes or earthquakes

How can you miss papercuts and burns

Scrapes and bruises

How can you miss the tears and stains,

Thoughts consuming you

Not being able to sleep for the fear of dreams-

No, *nightmares.*

How can you miss confusion, hatred, anger, rage, sadness, pity, loathing?

The longing looks met with a blank gaze,

The unreciprocated effort or the letters never returned, only read,

Is it normal to miss it?

To want it?

I miss you, I send.

Because you can miss the disasters, the ruin, the pain,

For isn't there always a calm before the storm?

And perhaps after the storm?

- **The Calm Before the Storm**

Xenization

It's funny how we walk past eachother

With an entire world between us

When last night

You were my world

And I yours

-    *The act of existing as a stranger*

Capax Infinity

"I can hold the world in my hands."

Capax Infinity, an astral sanctuary,

Held in hands, like a celestial emissary.

Capax Infinity, a universe whispers,

Symbols etched like celestial slippers.

Expressions dance, seasons come and go,

In the visage, a universe to know.

His face is a canvas painted, colours unfurled;

in its silent language, he is the world.

A world I hold within my palms

- Holding the infinite

Apricity

There's a beauty, a cold affair.

In the sharp bite of winter's wind

Huddled in warm clothes,

Eyes barely seen under scarfs and caps

My hands froze inside my jacket as I moved them to grab yours

It's too cold to keep them out,

I complained

Your fingers, a lifeline in the chill,

My pocket a poor substitute, still.

The small heatwaves rushing out of them into mine

Or maybe my entire body was heating up anyway with him next

to me

Come here, he said and pulled me close,

Slipping both our hands into his jacket

What a sight we must've looked like

But the snow didn't care; neither did the frost on the trees or the

breeze nipping at my nose.

And when you glanced at me again

It was warm enough to forget the world freezing around us

\-   *the warmth of the sun in winter*

Collywobbles

What a daft word

What an amazing feeling

butterflies in the stomach

The butterflies that dance a fluttering sequence,

A sensation that leaves nothing to chance.

With each step closer, their wings unfold,

A dance of feelings, precious and bold.

Butterflies, the poets of affection

- *butterflies in the stomach*

Σε αγαπώ περισσότερο κάθε μέρα

Everyone deserves someone who will

Text you random facts from their day

The most useless simple encounters

Just to have a reason to speak to you

- *I love you more every day*

Arisha Anne Bhattaharya

La Folie Dissimulée

Veiled in love's embrace,

Madness hides in elegance,

Heart's clandestine dance

a sense of concealing or disguising madness with a touch of

elegance

Risus abundat in ore stultorum

Your lips matched mine

Everyone saw it as we walked in

Words spoken in kisses, a language so divine,

In that shared moment, your lips matched mine

Let them know who owns your words

- *Laughter is abundant in the mouth of fools*

Arcane

How crazy to believe

That the only secrets kept to me,

the deepest, darkest ones

that I keep hidden in that little black box encased within my chest.

You hold it in your palm

Only for those I trust the most,

Whose voices aren't now a comforting boast.

Secrets meant for ears close and dear,

Not for those whose whispers I fear.

A chosen few are granted access to the innermost sanctum,

Where these clandestine truths linger, etched upon the heart.

It was a source of solace, a joy to be known

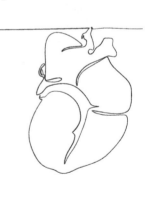

As intimately as you once knew me.

Yet now,

I yearn for a simpler acquaintance,

Where the only recognition you possess of me

Is encapsulated in the simplicity of my name.

- *known or understood by very few; mysterious; secret;*

  obscure; esoteric

Omne initium difficile est

For us to be strangers now

Oh how I wish we had started like that, too

Left it with a "Hello."

And never furthermore

- *Every beginning is difficult*

Omnes una manet nox

I would smile at you in the mornings

As if I didn't cry for you in the nights

You'd never know the redness in my eyes

The makeup I made up to match my blush

The quiver in my voice from the "cold"

The tiredness from "working too late"

How foolish of you

To not be able to see through the mist of lies

Telling you how happy I was at dawn

And wishing it to be all over by dusk

- *The same night awaits us all*

Prelapsarian

In the falling sands of an hourglass

The slow ticks from beside my head are inching their way

through the walls

Like the heartbeat I'd never hear.

I watch as time passes

In the prelapsarian echoes, a longing sigh,

To pause the narrative, to rewrite the script,

Undo the moments where innocence slipped.

And how I wish for it to stop

Oh, how I yearn for it to stall,

Just for a moment

To run back to myself and stop the inevitable

To halt the inevitable, a daring feat,

Unraveling the threads where destiny and past meet

- *a state of innocence or bliss before a significant event or fall from*

  grace

Sometimes

I'm willing to put in so much effort for someone

Not because I expect it from them,

But it's what I'd do within a heartbeat

So why won't you?

- ***Effort***

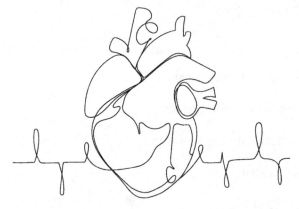

Arisha Anne Bhattaharya

Quisling

It hurt so much that

I started believing I deserved it

But what a disgusting world to live in

Where people's love

Has been made into an icicle

Stabbed and melted to seem useless

As if all the pain was a facade

The water is the most slightly tinged in red,

Just like your hands

When they squeezed my heart raw

And blamed it on me

- *Someone who has lost your confidence; traitor*

Cras es noster

In the darkest hours of the night

To read back what used to be

Only to wake up to the blinding light of what is

Makes me glad I've deleted traces of us

- *Tomorrow, be ours*

Tacenda

Sometimes, I wish to knock.

To call your name out in the dark,

To text you in the middle of the night

To grab your arm when no one's around

To smile when you're looking only at me

To say a thousand thoughts, I held back because I *couldn't say-*

Because I was *scared.*

Scared of what you'd say,

Of what it would end

Either the loneliness and heartache

Or *us*, our friendship, or whatever you claim we are

Suspended in this weird bubble in time,

Popping when others are around,

Perfectly intact when the only souls are you and me

The sound of waves crashing,

My nails on the screen

Or the sound of the creek

Those are the times when I wish everything unravelled around us

And the dam of secrets I hold within me can burst out.

No matter what it destroys in its path

- *things better left unsaid or matters that are to be passed over in silence*

Arisha Anne Bhattaharya

Μόνη σιγή μεταμέλειαν ου φέρει

Nothing speaks louder than the silence between us

No words can replace the pitch-black nothingness that stands

between us

Everyone can see it:

The absence of my presence around you

The disconnect between our jokes, answering with a question

when asked about the other

The awkward glances in each other's direction

We used to laugh, share dreams in sync,

Now, responses feel like a missing link

As if you wouldn't have fought for me,

A week ago, in a different reality

Ignoring my existence, once a cherished plea,

Now a cruel gesture, as if love has set free.

Ignoring my being as if it were a ghost,

A bond now severed, once held so close.

If silence reigns louder than the beating heart,

Then love's demise tears the soul apart.

Now, the silence speaks louder than you know.

-   *Silence alone is not an apology*

I can keep a secret.

I can keep a secret like no one can

Sly lies, quick turns, averted gazes

It's an art, to be able to hide my intentions

To deprieve oneself of their wants,

A million words on my tongue, bold.

Waiting to drop, yet never falling,

A cliffhanger, on the edge, enthralling.

I mean,

For you to never know how I felt

I must've been able to keep a secret damn well

Abscondō

I always thought I'd miss the version of

myself that had you

But now I'm missing the version of myself

that never knew you at all

- *To secretly depart and hide oneself*

Abience

Shying away from a matter never works out

Eyes never meeting, a silence, a doubt.

Not because of circumstance but forced swivels of my head as yours search for mine.

Turning my phone over as it vibrates on my desk,

Choosing to leave the room rather than read it,

Skim the words of disgust you pose at my latest comment

Perhaps avoiding the situation never works out,

Avoiding the person might be the next best thing

A dance of evasions, a carefully crafted play,

To distance ourselves, to keep feelings at bay

Yet, sometimes abience is a shield,

A refuge from wounds yet to be healed.

A temporary respite from the storm,

A chance to find a safer, gentler norm.

- *an urge to withdraw or avoid a situation or an object*

Solamen miseris socios habuisse doloris

Your absence doesn't scare me

As much as the relief that comes from it

If I am so fine with you leaving now

Why did I hold on so hard to begin with

- *Misery loves company*

Cogitationes cordis

Tell me everything on your mind.

Spill your darkest thoughts,

Stain my white shirt until it's covered in blood-red wine,

Soak it till I'll carry your scent wherever I go

Tell me anything that burdens you

Get it off your chest,

Breathe again

Give it all to me,

All the pain, suffering, burdens

Even if I have to carry it forever

I'd live with your lies forever as long as your truth sticks

with me, too

- *Thoughts of the heart*

Iubirea mea

Call me anything

Call me darling, sweetheart, baby, dear,

My love, honey, angel, babe,

Call me your bro, your homie, your best friend

Call me your soulmate, your girlfriend, your future wife

Call me by my name,

Call me by *yours*

Just don't leave me in silence,

Where the only sounds from your lips are caught in

time,

And my name ceases to exist
- *My love*

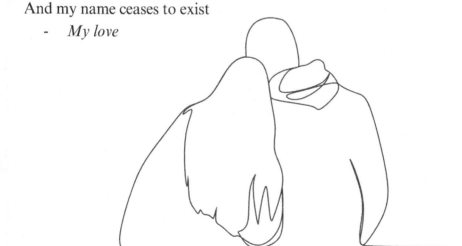

Φιλία εστί μία ψυχή εν δυσί σώμασιν ενοικουμένη

People forget how much love is in friendships

To be able to bond your soul to another

Even far,

Though there is space in distance

Never in heart

- *Friendship is one soul living in two bodies.*

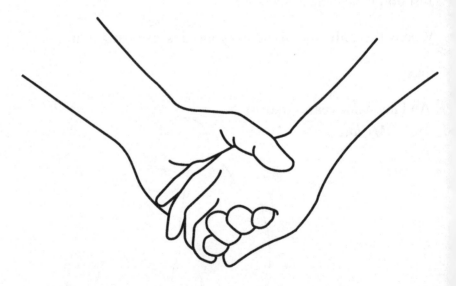

-

Jamais cesser de le dire

People don't say my name correctly.

They pronounced it well, and technically, it wasn't wrong

But I never realised how right it sounded from your lips

Even now, in a hundred voices

A thousand screams and shouts,

A million whispers, I'll hear you

Say it again and again till I'm sick of it

Tumbling from your lips into mine,

Into my neck, my hair, as you hold me close,

Into my ears as you laugh at my cheeks hotten

Into your phone as we whisper goodnight

I love how you say my name

- *Never stop saying it*

Felix Culpa

I wish you could see the stupid smile on my face

Whenever your name pops up on my screen

- *happy fault*

Arisha Anne Bhattaharya

Lethologica

People always say I have a way with words,

Never at a loss for a quick quip, a sarcastic remark, an encouraging word

or a sweet anecdote Describing hatred, envy, disgust, anger, fear

Describing happiness, comfort, serenity, peace, joy

These come easily

But what is the word to describe

Not knowing where we stand,

A ballet of uncertainty, a fleeting trance

A sense of confusion after each parting, yet-

Being completely unable to breathe every time you step closer

A sense of shock when your eyes meet mine, yet-

My nails mark my palms when I see you with her

Knowing the way you spoke mere minutes ago to me

A sense of betrayal, of disappointment, when no action ensued from the

repetition of the past, yet-

Wanting, no, needing to glimpse your shaggy hair in a crowd, see you

smile each day, your picture show up on my screen, your voice ring

through the room

A sense of love whenever your presence is nearby

What word is that?

To describe this whole plethora of emotions that completely envelop a

person

Is there one at all, or should I call it your name?

- *the inability to remember a particular word or name.*

Lacrimae rerum

When I remember your name

I smile

I smile when I think about your face,

Your smile, your laugh

The image of your text popping up on my screen

I smile through it all because it brings me joy

If joy, then why does your vision blur?

Why do your eyes fog up,

Your fingers are wet when they reach your cheeks

Moments of joy framed in liquid pain

Is that joy?

Your name, a melody in laughter's chord,

Yet, why does joy carry a tear-stained sword?

- *The tears of things*

Ataraxia

You ask me what I'm thinking,

But how does one describe the pure happiness that my mind feels around
you

There are no thoughts beyond the colour of your eyes, the heat radiating
off your skin so near that it burns me

Nothing I can express to show utter tranquillity

Everything once troubling now a blank screen

You ask me why my eyes seem far away,

My voice devoid of words, left for a smile

that will never leave around you

"What's going on in that mind of yours?"

I say nothing

All I can do is smile

- *state of inner peace and calmness, free from*
  disturbances and anxieties

Aubade

Light doesn't just disappear.

As the sun gradually dips under the mountains

So I saw your love slowly fade

The inevitable folly of time that I never believed would come

Just as you wish your birthday never to end,

Counting each second, wishing time to sit still

So did I with our past

A timeline set before we even met,

Doomed to always end in a day and rise the next

With only the moon's light being a beacon of hope between those

cold hours of dusk and tears And the delusions mixed with streaks

of sunlight in the dawn

Now I hate watching sunrises

Knowing they will end in sunsets

- *song that greets the dawn*

Timeo Danaos et dona ferentes

Stop lying to yourself about who a person is

They know who they are

It's about time you starting accepting them for their actions too

- *I fear Greeks even if they bring gifts.*

Kalopsia

Waiting for someone to change

Doesn't ever truly change how they act

It just changes how you feel

All the waiting leads to allowance,

Accountability leads to excuses

And change never really means change,

It means time for you to accept the facts of life,

And hopefully never hope for a person to change for you

Because someone who truly means to become better

Will never leave you waiting for them to act different.

- *delusion of things being more beautiful than they really are*

Όρα το μέλλον

There's no bigger war

Than walking away from someone you love

But will never respect again

For the heart may yearn for more

But the imprint of your hand on my cheek

A fortune teller could read it

And tell me we aren't meant to be together

-   *Keep sight of the future.*

Sphallolalia

A playful banter, a teasing exchange,

A mirage of connection, an elusive range.

a linguistic play where the journey itself becomes the destination

a delightful ambiguity that leaves room for imagination to roam,

Feeding me delusions

Of hope, of something to look forward to

But perhaps

Late nights spent in the exchange of laughter,

subtle hair tucks,

Touch of our lips,

caresses of the back

Are all signs of friendship?

Tell me, did you never mean for this to be,

More than the warmth of companionship, just a plea?

- *flirting that leads nowhere*

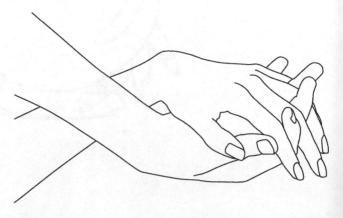

Inima mea plânge în tăcere pentru ceea ce am pierdut.

Being in love doesn't mean looking over one's inadequacies

It doesn't mean ignoring the bad or making excuses for the

wrongdoings It means letting your heart care even when your

brain is angry

Should there ever be a moment where

Your heart stops caring when you hurt me

That's when the love has been lost,

Not when my heart still aches for you throughout all the pain

For in the silence of a heart withdrawn,

The sweetest symphony may be gone.

And as the final notes in sorrow are tossed,

That's when love laments, for it may be lost.

- My heart weeps in silence for what I have lost

Si Vis Amari, Ama

"I wish I was easier to love."

Everyone is easy to love because love doesn't depend on the person.

Knows no prerequisites, no conditions,

The amount of love given

Is the amount of love had

To give is to possess, a reciprocal dance,

So, never believe you can't be loved

For if a person has nothing inside their heart to give

It's not your job to make it up for them

Easier or not, to love oneself truly,

In the vast expanse, love finds you.

- *If you wish to be loved, love*

Lux Brumalis

If you ever feel like you're losing it all

That everything has left you

Don't forget the trees

That lose all their leaves

The flowers that lose their petals

Lose all their beauty and life

Just to grow it all back next spring

You will grow from this winter

Spring will be here before you know it

- *the light of winter*

Post hoc, ergo propter hoc

Who you will become someday

Depends on what you heal from today

- *After this, therefore because of this*

Anaxiphilia

I'm never mad at someone's actions

That their character

Be you

Be your character, your mindsets and personas

But sometimes you can't deal with a character anymore

It's not anger, not a condemnation,

But an acknowledgement that the script has shifted.

The realization dawns that it's time,

Time to turn the pages, to explore new chapters,

And realize it's time to move on to the next book

- *an act of falling in love with the wrong person*

Redamancy

You can't make a person love you

All you can do is love them

And see what they decide to do with that love

- *the act of loving the one who loves you; a love returned in full*

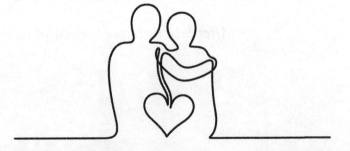

Maudlin

I still remember the joke he made on the first day of school,

cracking up so hard our sides split

Or the sour candy I eat every thanksgiving because my brother

loved it

The red shirt I wear on special occasions because my best friend

loved the color on me

The french song I listen to late at night because he sung it to me

And the dances my friend's brother taught me the one instance

we met

I live through everything the people I love have loved before me

For I am a mosaic

Of my old loves

- *foolishly sentimental*

दया लनी

Perhaps we were only a chapter in each others' lives

What must I now do

With the empty library sitting their

Waiting to hold all our books?

- *Residing in the heart*

Εσύ είσαι η ιστορία που η καρδιά μου θέλει να ζήσει

Gifting books is the most romantic gesture ever done

To be giving an entire life

To be giving a narrative they will love

Your inscriptions drawn inside,

Sweet notes of love as they open the words you've scoured

Isn't it beautiful?

To gift a book is to give a piece of oneself,

A shared universe where emotions delve.

In the quiet act of passing on a loved tome,

Lies a sentiment that transcends, a love poem.

- *You are the story my heart wants to live*

Aere Perrenius

I wish to explore you forever

To read every story you have

Spend eternity between your pages

Like the Library of Alexandria

Had it not burnt down

Leaving only cinders of what used to be

- *more lasting than bronze*

-

Wistoragic

I love how you give me the longest books

Only to end our story so quick

lingering sadness and nostalgia after the end of a series or story

Do you think I'd come running to you

Arms open, all forgiven,

Memory wiped as if I didn't try to yank the thoughts of you out

physically?

Running to you with a smile on my face,

Only to meet an empty street,

A locked door, a voicemail

A letter never returned, a smile never reciprocated

A nasty word, an accusation, a threat

Did you think I'd run to you only to get hit back

As if you were a cliff, the sharp rocks at the bottom being half as

sharp as your tone.

Who launches a spaceship towards a black hole?

Maybe there's hope for exploration and discovery

But it's futile: a journey with no return and no hope for survival

How could I run towards that?

Why would I run towards that again?

Instead, take the other route:

The scenic one, the safe one,

Or don't leave home for a promise made with your fingers crosses

I won't ever come running again,

For who runs into a dead end?

- ***Running To You***

Stropii de ploaie cad ca lacrimi ale cerului mâhnit

I wish I were like thunderstorms

Nature's way of screaming through it's pain and sadness

I wish I were like a typhoon

Raining everything down, releasing all of it in one go

Emptying the clouds of its weight in tears, pouring down

until everything feels wet and moist

No sign of dryness or exhaustion

Just the dewiness of fresh beginnings

Instead, I fear to be like tsunamis

Pulling back, isolation and detachment

Only to flood everything I once loved in my path when it all

comes inevitably crashing down.

Should sadness not be gradual?

Why must it be a crash of a wave instead of a steady tide?

- *Raindrops fall like the sorrowful tears of the sky.*

Arisha Anne Bhattacharya

Videre veritatem

Somewhere along the way,

I stopped hoping for more

It hit me like the first drop of rain on ur nose

Knowing that one instance wouldn't stop with that

It's merely a warning for the storm lying ahead

After the hundredth time,

Waking up to a wet pillow, puffy eyes and a cold heart

I realised it

How could you change?

Unless a sudden epiphany hits you:

A train, a tsunami, an asteroid

Until it hit you so hard that your world changed

You wouldn't change

Saying sorry again and again

And seeing no difference isn't an apology

It's an excuse

So why should I make excuses for you when those are all you

give me?

\-   *To see the truth*   **Ex nihilo nihil fit**

I will never be your second choice again

Not when you've always been my first

\- *Nothing comes from nothing*

Ephemeral

They leave and act like it never happened

Only to return like they never left

They depart, as if erased by time,

Only to reappear, like an unwritten rhyme.

- *Lasting for a very short time; fleeting*

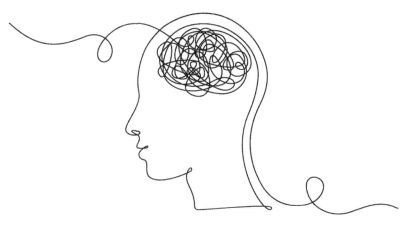

Mea culpa

You see a person's true colors

When they get mad about the truth

Or perhaps

Get mad at the version of truth they never wanted to see

The version that hurt you

- *Through my fault*

Alexithymia

The inability to express or identify emotions,

How ironic of a word, and even more ironic of a timing

How can one not express their emotions,

Perhaps if you didn't know,

Blinded by hubris and perspectives not shared

But what excuse could be given

When the emotions are thrown in your face?

Is ignorance, defiance, and arguing a valid response?

All because emotions were felt,

No, not just felt,

Because emotions were expressed

How unfair,

To be blamed just for feeling things.

- *emotional blindness*

Πάντων των αναγκαίων κακών ιατρός χρόνος εστίν

I feel sick when I remember all you know about me

Why should a disease have access to my heart?

- *Time is the healer of all inevitable ills*

Veni Vidi Amavi

La pauvre, aveuglée par l'amour

In the gentle shadow of the stars,

Une âme perdue, blinded by love,

Sinks into the darkness of dreams,

Où les étincelles du cœur brillent encore.

Embraced by passion, elle danse,

In the meanders of illusions,

Son regard, veiled with tender emotion,

Explore a world drunk on seduction.

Les étoiles whisper love's refrains,

Weaving dreams in the ethereal night,

But captivated by fervor's chains,

Elle ne voit que l'éclat de la lumière égarée.

Red roses bloom in the shadow's caress,

Stroking the dreams of a sincere embrace,

Yet, dazzled by the dark flame's finesse,

Elle s'éloigne sur le chemin de la grâce lumineuse.

Love's shards blind her searching gaze,

Passionate embrace, both sweet and bitter,

Wandering lost in the darkened maze,

Son cœur captif de l'éclat éphémère de l'amour.

Intoxicated by heaven's promises so divine,

Truth and falsehood, elle fails to define,

Son cœur captif d'un amour profond,

Vagabonde vulnérable dans les ténèbres, déliée.

Thus, perdue dans la nuit sinueuse,

Elle recherche la clarté dans l'absence de lumière,

Pourtant, love, tendre bourreau si doux,

L'aveugle, la guidant vers la splendeur infinie.

Blinded by love, elle continues to dance,

In the obscurité de l'étendue étoilée,

Son cœur, une mélodie d'une transe passionnée,

Rêve d'un amour éternel, d'une chance de coexistence.

- *blinded by love*

Songs to fall back in love to:

♥

42. Friends–Chase Atlantic

43. Line Without a Hook–Ricky Montgomery

44. Freaks–Surf Curse

45. To Build A Home - The Cinematic Orchestra

46. we fell in love in october–girl in red

47. Something About You - Eyedress

48. Love In The Dark–Adele

49. Thousand Years - Christina Perri

50. Riptide - Vance Joy

51. Yes To Heaven - Lana Del Ray

52. Always Forever - Cults

53. Love Grows - Edison Lighthouse

54. Heart To Heart–Mac DeMarco

55. From The Start–Laufey

56. Radio–Lana Del Rey

57. This Side of Paradise–Coyote Theory

58. Make You Mine–Danielle Bradbery and PUBLIC

Acknowledgements

♥

To be perfectly honest, I'd never written poetry enough to want to publish it, yet sometimes, when our emotions become undeniably beautiful, to the brink of pain and ecstasy, perhaps it's good enough to show to the world. Written in just seven days, this is a collection of thoughts, memories, fantasies and regrets, a sliver of a testimony to my version of love. Though not the first book I thought to be published, it's still such a massive moment for me as a writer, and I hope this is the first of many to come. Some are raw, some are sad, some are happy, and some are just a window into my life. I hope you enjoy this book the way I enjoyed writing it.

With every emotion in the universe.

I'd like to firstly thank Mama and Papa, who, though not even knowing what I was writing about, stood behind me and gave me the utmost support in the short life of its publication. Mama, for never once saying no to my obsession with reading, always taking me to bookstores, helping me walk out with a stack taller than myself. You're the reason I will ever write, the reason I hope to make as much of a difference with my books as other authors have done to me.

Acknowledgements

To Papa, for teaching me to chase my aspirations in life. You showed me that anything is possible through all the fantastic things you've accomplished–all it takes is hard work and time. To Aarav, whom I promised to publish a book a verryyyy long time ago, who always proofread my work, giving your little criticisms and praise–you made this so worth it. This is just the beginning, and I hope to sign a hundred more for you. To my cousin Mishu and my best friend Ai, who heard every story, voice memo, and long text, listened to my dreams and rants a thousand times–I love you guys for lending an ear and a heart. No matter how far away, you still make me feel your presence beside me each day.

To my girls: Anya, Yashika, and Jojo, for standing by my side, for a million hugs, encouraging words, tough talks, and shoulders to lean on. For hyping me up on my low days, going out and having fun on the best, being an even better outlet than my books, crafting a more beautiful life than any pen.

. Through a crazy year, I'm so grateful to have had you guys by my side through thick and thin.

Acknowledgements

❤

Josh, for always giving me the most down-to-earth life lessons yet being my biggest hype man ever. I am not sure what daft nonsense I'd get up to without your advice.

Nithila and Janie, for always being by my side through the weird, ridiculous late-night calls and class gossip sessions–I honestly don't know how you put up with me, but I love y'all for it. For feeding into my delusions and keeping me grounded simultaneously, my guardian angels every day.

To Alex, thank you for making me love poetry so much; I truly couldn't have written this book without your inspiration.

And finally, to *you*, dear reader. I hope you always live life by feeling everything, all the daft stoops and highs of love, for the world would be such a bleak place if we didn't let our emotions run wild every now and then.

- yours truly,
Arisha Anne Bhattacharya<3

Made in the USA
Las Vegas, NV
27 January 2024

84927663R00083